# The Tail of the Whale

Written by Ellie Patterson & illustrated by Christine Pym

meadowside
CHILDREN'S BOOKS

When winter days
are cold and grey,
When frost lies on the ground,

When all the colours wash away,
And rainbows can't be found,

When people shiver, branches quiver,
And everything looks bland,
I like to slip away into a multi-coloured land!

Deep below the dark blue sea,
We dip and dive and dart,

Down we go -
now hold on tight...

The show's
about to start!

Underneath the swelling sea
Where people seldom go,

A kaleidoscope of fishes dance
a psychedelic show!

# Roll up, roll up,
## the fish parade!

Where colours come in every shade!
They swim between your little toes
And shimmer past your very nose!

And here it comes, the main event...

So this is where
the colours went!

A shoal of shining rainbow fish
In every colour you could wish!
They dart and dash,
        so bold and bright...

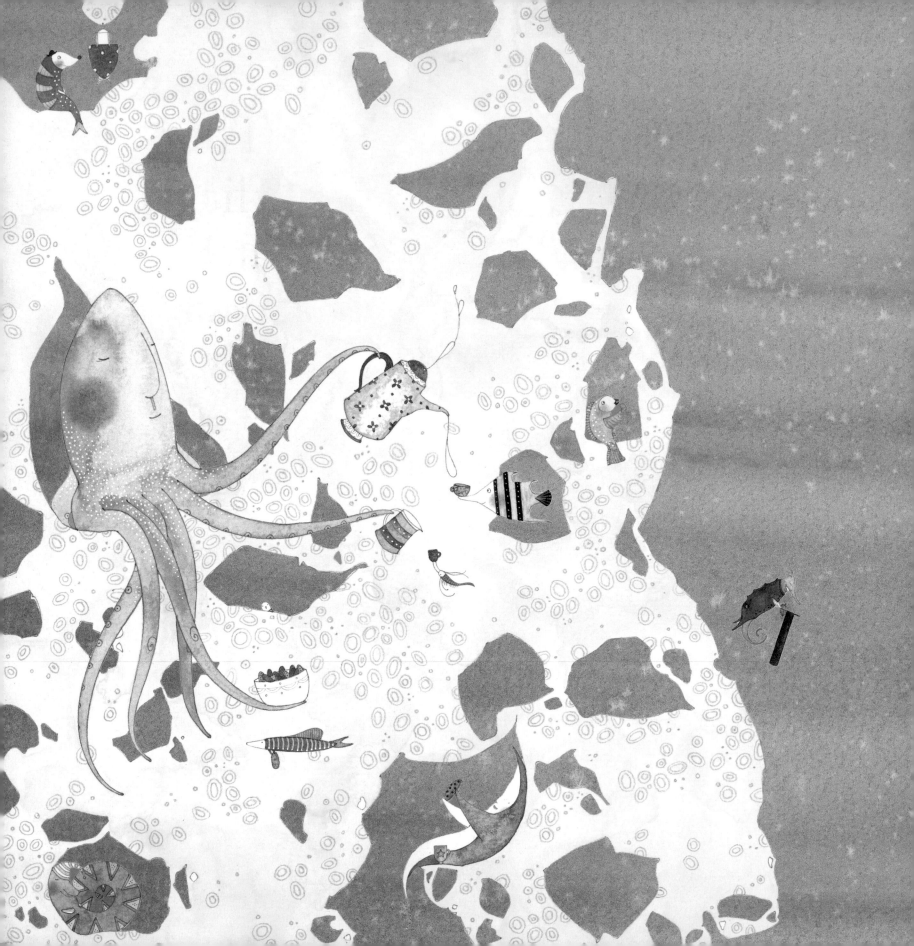

As coral curtains mark the end,
It's time to leave the show
Of rainbows dancing in the sea,
Where all the colours go.

All aboard the great whale's tail!
We're heading back up top,

Where everything is dull and bland...

But wait a minute... stop!

The world looks very different now,
It glistens in the light,

Happy laughter fills the air,
The blue sky shines
so bright.

The colours underneath the sea were really quite a show,
But nothing makes me smile quite like the sight...

...of white, white snow!

To Mum and Dad
and all the parents who read to
their children before bed

E.P.

To my mum and dad
for helping me and more xx

C.P.

First published in 2008
by Meadowside Children's Books
185 Fleet Street
London EC4A 2HS
www.meadowsidebooks.com

Text © Ellie Patterson
Illustrations © Christine Pym
The rights of Ellie Patterson and Christine Pym
to be identified as the author and illustrator of this work
have been asserted by them in accordance with the
Copyright, Designs and Patents Act, 1988

A CIP catalogue record for this book
is available from the British Library
10 9 8 7 6 5 4 3 2

Printed in China